Itzel AND THE Ocelot

Itzel
AND THE
Ocelot

Rachel Katstaller

Kids Can Press

Many, many years ago, although it might have been yesterday, a little girl named Itzel lived with her nana at the edge of the jungle.

Itzel loved nothing more than to listen to her nana's stories and to play the flute her grandfather had made for her.

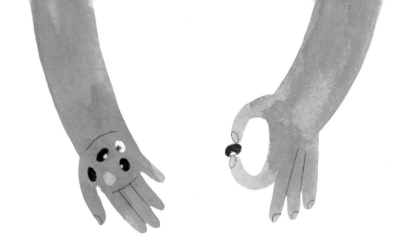

The year of our story, a long dry spell had plagued the country, and not one drop of rain had fallen from the sky.

Itzel and her nana needed rain to water the seeds they had planted together. Their stores of corn, beans and squash were running low. Her nana would soon have nothing to sell at the market. And worse, they would have nothing to eat.

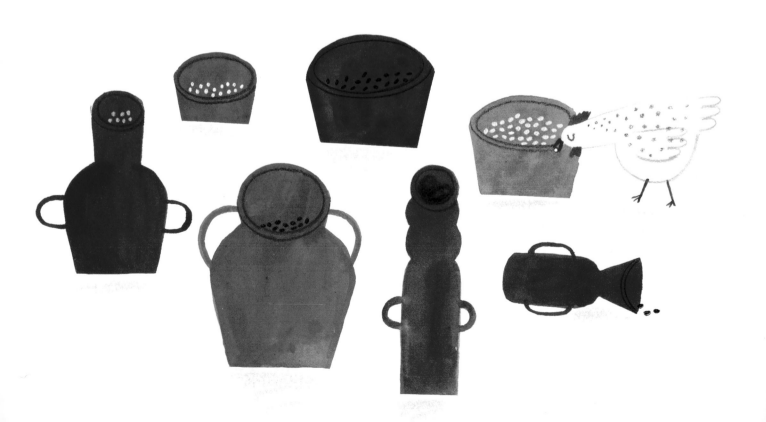

At night, as the fresh breeze cooled them, Itzel swung
in the hammock and her nana told her favorite story.

"When the earth was newly born," her nana began,
"the lords of the hills would awaken the giant snake from
its deep sleep. First with a whisper, and then with a deep
thunderous cry, the giant snake would bring the arrival of
the rainy season."

"Nana, why have I never seen the giant snake?" Itzel asked.

"Many do not believe in it anymore. So it has returned to the place where the water is born," answered her nana.

"Goodness, how long will we have to wait for this rain?" Her nana sighed impatiently. Itzel offered her a sip of atol.

"No, my child, you eat, I'm already full," she said, even though Itzel could hear her nana's stomach grumble.

If only Itzel could do something! Could she find and awaken the giant snake herself?

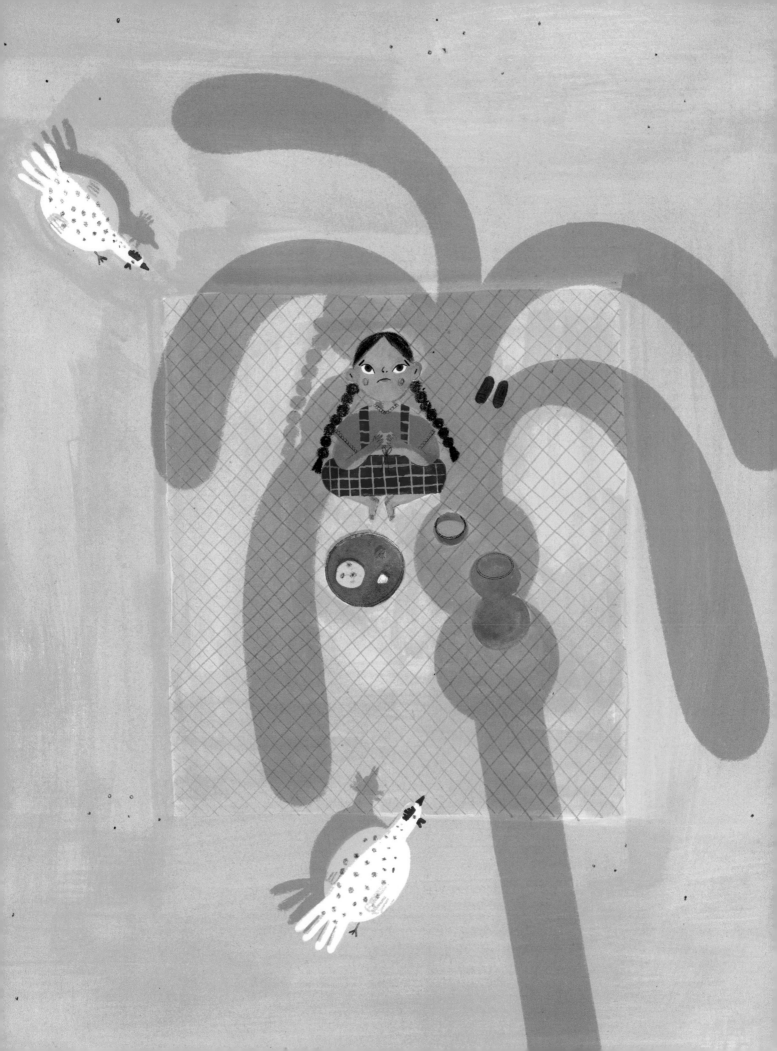

That night, as her nana slept deeply, Itzel took her flute and
left home in search of the river and the mysterious giant snake.

The full moon cast deep shadows teeming with threatening shapes.

Itzel felt her way through the trees but then, all at once,

she lost her footing and plunged down,

tumbling and tumbling

deep into the jungle.

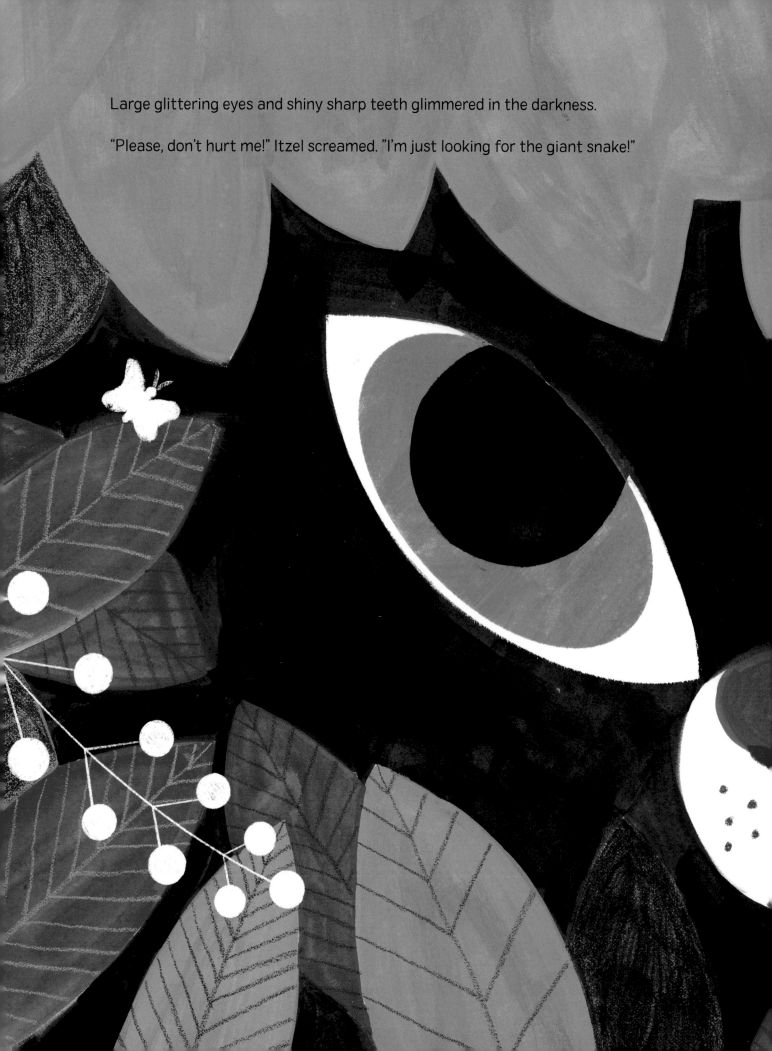

Large glittering eyes and shiny sharp teeth glimmered in the darkness.

"Please, don't hurt me!" Itzel screamed. "I'm just looking for the giant snake!"

After several heartbeats, Itzel opened her eyes. An ocelot
was staring right at her.

"You know about the giant snake?" he asked.

"You can *speak*?" Itzel was amazed.

"All animals can speak, but you humans never listen," he
said. "Why are you looking for the giant snake?"

"I need it to bring us water for our crops!"

"I'm thirsty myself. I guess I could help…" The ocelot
gestured for Itzel to follow him deeper into the jungle.

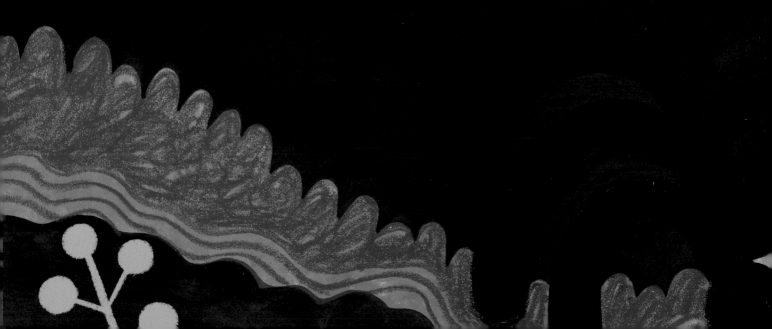

Crack, crunch, creak ...

From afar, Itzel saw an opossum trying to shape a comal.
The clay was too dry and the comal kept breaking in half.

"Why don't you come with us to search for the giant
snake?" Itzel asked.

"The giant snake doesn't exist!" the opossum snorted.
"But ... it wouldn't hurt to look, just to make sure."

The three marched on.

Next, Itzel saw a toothy creature crying next to a spindly tree.

Concerned, she asked, "Do you also need the giant snake to bring back the rain?"

"The giant snake!" the agouti scoffed.

"I'm going to find it at the river," Itzel said.

The agouti wiped the tears from her eyes. "I need water for my tree to grow enough huacales to sell at the market. So if you're going to find water, I might as well join you."

On they walked, winding through deep shadows and moonlight streaming in through the boughs.

Suddenly, Itzel stopped — she had run into a funny creature hanging down by her long tail.

"Are you all right?" Itzel asked.

"Yes," the kinkajou said. "But my children aren't! They are waiting for me to bring water, and there is none to be found!"

"Would you like to come look for the giant snake with us?" Itzel offered.

"Well, we can at least try," the kinkajou said, looking unsure but following along.

More animals joined Itzel in her search for the giant snake. Even though they didn't believe they would find it, all needed water. Itzel pressed on, determined to prove the giant snake's existence.

Something was shining beyond the trees. Was this the place where the water is born? Had Itzel been right all along?

All the creatures held their breath ...

But there was *nothing* there! The riverbed was dry.

Heartbroken, Itzel realized the truth. She had given these creatures false hope. There was no giant snake and no water, and the seeds her nana had planted would never grow! Itzel hadn't been able to save them.

She sat down and started playing her flute. As tears ran down her cheeks, the creatures cried with her.

BOOM!

CRASH!

ROAR!

From underneath them, a long shadow
sprang into the sky. The riverbed surrounding
them starting to fill up with water.

Itzel and the ocelot held on to each other as a wave from the rising river lifted them up, carrying them downstream. Along the banks of the river, the other animals began their journey home.

On the way down, they waved goodbye to the
other creatures. The kinkajou looked pleased as she
cooked breakfast for her children.

"Thank you!" said the agouti, cheerfully watering
her tree.

With dirty paws, the opossum waved a thankful
goodbye as he finished shaping the comal.

Finally, Itzel and the ocelot were home. They joined
her nana in the hammock to watch the rain fall.

Many, many years ago, although it might have been
yesterday, the world was set right again by a little girl
who had the courage to believe in the tales of old.

Glossary

You will probably have noticed several unfamiliar words in this story. They have roots in one of El Salvador's original languages, spoken before the Spanish came to this part of the world. This language is called Nawat. And many, many years ago, these words were adapted to Spanish. The glossary below lists the Spanish and Nawat words used in this story. For more information on the Nawat language, you can visit the Colectivo Tzunhejekat at http://tushik.org/english/what-is-nawat/.

agouti: a type of rodent related to the guinea pig and found in North, Central and South America

atol (Nawat: atul): a slightly sweet beverage made of white corn, served hot

comal (Nawat: kumal): a smooth, round griddle made of clay, used to cook tortillas or toast cacao beans

huacal (Nawat: wajwakal): a vessel made with the fruit of the huacal tree, also known as calabash tree

kinkajou: a tropical rain forest animal related to raccoons and native to Central and South America

nana (Nawat: nananoya): grandmother

Author's Note

As a half Austrian, half Salvadoran child, I grew up hearing many different stories that connected me to both my heritages. This book was inspired by the story of the giant snake, or cuyancuat, a creature said to have the head of a pig and the body of a snake. It lives near the rivers and announces the beginning of the rainy season with a cry that shakes the earth. This version of the story comes from the regions of Izalco and Santo Domingo de Guzmán.

But the story that I loved above all others was about the people who inhabited our country many hundreds of years ago and their tonales (from the Nahuatl word "tonalli," which means day or day sign). The tonales were protective spirits that took the shape of an animal. Human and animal were inseparable — if one died, so did the other. In this book, the ocelot is Itzel's tonal.

These stories have stuck with me for years, reminding me of the interconnectedness we humans have with the earth we live on. In these times, I believe it is of great importance to look back on these traditional stories because they help us understand how to have a good relationship with our planet. But these stories are also an essential part of our heritage, culture and identity. I hope this book is just the first of many stories from El Salvador that you get to explore.

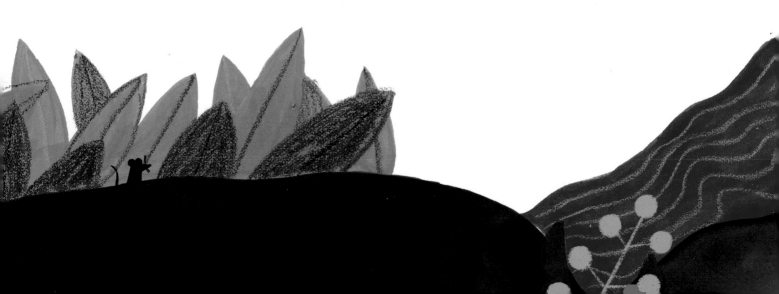

To my mother and grandmother, who love telling stories — R.K.

Acknowledgements

Thank you to my amazing agent, Abigail Samoun, and wonderful editor, Kathleen Keenan, for believing in this story. And a special thank you to my friend E. Dohle for sharing her resources on Nawat with me.

Text and illustrations © 2022 Rachel Katstaller

All rights reserved. No part of this publication may be reproduced, stored in a retrieval system or transmitted, in any form or by any means, without the prior written permission of Kids Can Press Ltd. or, in case of photocopying or other reprographic copying, a license from The Canadian Copyright Licensing Agency (Access Copyright). For an Access Copyright license, visit www.accesscopyright.ca or call toll free to 1-800-893-5777.

Published in Canada and the U.S. by Kids Can Press Ltd.
25 Dockside Drive, Toronto, ON M5A 0B5

Kids Can Press is a Corus Entertainment Inc. company.

www.kidscanpress.com

The artwork in this book was rendered using a combination of colored pencils, acrylic paints and gouache.
The text is set in Colby.

Edited by Kathleen Keenan
Designed by Marie Bartholomew

Printed and bound in Buji, Shenzhen, China, in 10/2021 by WKT Company

CM 22 0 9 8 7 6 5 4 3 2 1

FSC
www.fsc.org
MIX
Paper from
responsible sources
FSC® C010256

Library and Archives Canada Cataloguing in Publication

Title: Itzel and the Ocelot / Rachel Katstaller.
Names: Katstaller, Rachel, author, illustrator.
Description: Includes some text in Nawat.
Identifiers: Canadiana 20210214813 | ISBN 9781525305061 (hardcover)
Classification: LCC PR9298.9.K38 I89 2022 | DDC j823/.92 — dc23

Kids Can Press gratefully acknowledges that the land on which our office is located is the traditional territory of many nations, including the Mississaugas of the Credit, the Anishnabeg, the Chippewa, the Haudenosaunee and the Wendat peoples, and is now home to many diverse First Nations, Inuit and Métis peoples.

We thank the Government of Ontario, through Ontario Creates; the Ontario Arts Council; the Canada Council for the Arts; and the Government of Canada for supporting our publishing activity.